I Love You, Little One

NANCY TAFURI

SCHOLASTIC INC.

New York   Toronto   London   Auckland   Sydney
Mexico City   New Delhi   Hong Kong

ISBN 0-590-92208-4

Copyright © 1998 by Nancy Tafuri.
All rights reserved. Published by Scholastic Inc.
SCHOLASTIC and associated logos are trademarks and/or registered trademarks of Scholastic Inc.

12 11 10 9 8 7 6 5 4 3 2 1   9/9 0 1 2 3 4/0

Printed in U.S.A.   08

First Scholastic paperback printing, January 1999

Book design by David Saylor
The artwork was created with watercolor inks and colored pencils.
The text is set in 22-point Iowan Bold Italic.

For Cristina, my little one,
and for Lauren Thompson and Owen,
her little one

Deep in the woods
by the sandy riverbank,
a little deer asks,
"Do you love me, Mama?"

And Mama Deer says,
"Yes, little one,
I love you as the river loves you,
full and singing before you,
giving you cool water to drink.
I love you as the river loves you,
forever and ever and always."

Deep in the woods
by the mossy pond edge,
a little duck asks,
"Do you love me, Mama?"

And Mama Duck says,
"Yes, little one,
I love you as the pond loves you,
wide and calm beneath you,
giving you food and places to swim.
I love you as the pond loves you,
forever and ever and always."

Deep in the woods
in a dirt-dug burrow,
a little rabbit asks,
"Do you love me, Mama?"

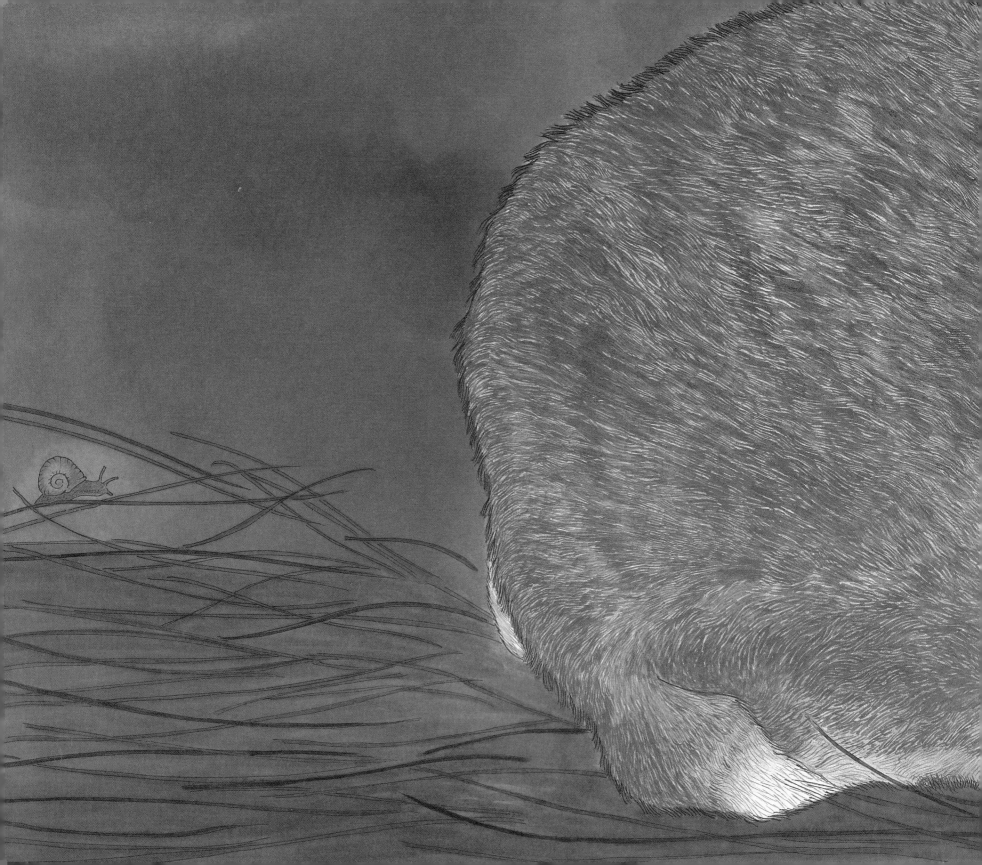

And Mama Rabbit says,
"Yes, little one,
I love you as the earth loves you,
cozy and snug around you,
giving you a warm place to sleep.
I love you as the earth loves you,
forever and ever and always."

Deep in the woods
in a grassy meadow,
a little mouse asks,
"Do you love me, Mama?"

And Mama Mouse says,
"Yes, little one,
I love you as the wild rye loves you,
gently swaying above you,
giving you food and cover from harm.
I love you as the wild rye loves you,
forever and ever and always."

Deep in the woods
in a dark mountain cave,
a little bear asks,
"Do you love me, Mama?"

And Mama Bear says,
"Yes, little one,
I love you as the mountain loves you,
sturdy and safe around you,
giving you shelter from snow and rain.
I love you as the mountain loves you,
forever and ever and always."

Deep in the woods
in an oak tree hollow,
a little owl asks,
"Do you love me, Mama?"

And Mama Owl says,
"Yes, little one,
I love you as the oak tree loves you,
tall and strong beside you,
giving you the world to see all around.
I love you as the oak tree loves you,
forever and ever and always."

Deep in the woods
in a log-built house,
a little child asks,
"Do you love me, Mama?"

And Mama says,
"Yes, little one,
I love you as the stars love you,
constant and bright above you,
giving you joy and peace and wonder.
I love you as the stars love you,
                    forever,
                        and ever,
                        and always."